This one is for the wolf, and for grandmothers in their power...
—HW

To my husband, Marcelo, who inspires my creativity,
to my young daughter, Beatriz, who has already changed my life forever,
and to my parents for their great support.
—RA

ILLUMINATION
Arts

PUBLISHING COMPANY, INC.
Bellevue, Washington

Little Ruth Reddingford
and the Wolf

An old tale retold by Hank Wesselman, Ph.D.

Illustrated by Raquel Abreu

This is the story of little Ruth Reddingford. Because of her name and the color of her hair, everyone called her Red. She even had a red poncho with a hood, just like the girl in another story.

On Saturdays when her parents were at work, Red loved to visit Grandma at her condo. They always had a great time singing, telling stories, putting on teddy bear tea parties, and taking long walks in the woods.

Red especially liked hearing tales about her great grandmother who had been a Hopi medicine woman.

One Saturday, Red was all ready to go when the phone rang. "Good morning, dear," said Grandma. "I'm sorry I won't be able to see you today. My car wouldn't start, so I can't pick you up."

Red was old enough to stay home alone, but her heart was set on having a picnic with Grandma. *I know a shortcut through the woods,* she thought. *I'll make a lunch and surprise Grandma!*

Red packed a bag with radishes and carrots, Grandma's favorites. Then she added granola bars and apples, her favorites, plus a few other goodies. After writing her mom a note, off she went.

The forest felt magical that morning. Birds were calling, bees were humming, woodpeckers were pecking, and blue dragonflies were zooming between the tall, dark trees. But suddenly, it became very quiet. *I don't remember the woods feeling so spooky when I was here with Grandma,* Red thought. *Is something watching me?*

Red was about to run when two boys jumped out from behind
a tree and tried to snatch her bag. She whirled around. It was Butch
and Spike, the school bullies!

Fortunately, Red was dodge ball champion of her class, so she was able to dance away from them.

"Hey, whatcha got in your bag?" Butch jeered.

"Let's make her eat worms," said Spike with a nasty laugh.

Clutching her bag, Red ran up the trail as fast as she could.

With the boys right behind her, Red dashed up the stairs
to Grandma's front porch. Out of breath, she was struggling to
open the door when Spike shoved her into the living room.

Butch grabbed her arm and twisted. "Now we're gonna see
what's in your bag."

"LET GO OF ME YOU BIG BULLY!" Red yelled in her
loudest, no-nonsense voice.

Just then Grandma appeared with the
Hopi throwing stick that had been her
grandmother's...and a large white wolf
glided silently into the room.

Four things happened right in a row:

First, Grandma threw her stick across the room, sending Butch sprawling.

Second, Spike tripped over Butch as he made a dash for the door.

Third, the wolf nipped Spike right on the seat of his
dirty shorts.

And fourth, Red picked up the phone and called 911.

Grandma had settled into her favorite chair by the time the sheriff arrived. "Funny," he said, scratching his head, "those boys were just sitting there shaking. Kept saying something about a big, mean dog, but I didn't see a thing."

As Red poured everyone tea, she winked at Grandma, who then told the sheriff what had happened… "and that's the story of a *good* wolf," she finished.

After the sheriff left, Grandma made a big plate of tacos, and
Red set up chairs for the teddy bear picnic. Grandma offered a taco to
each of the bears, and they were about to eat when the wolf reappeared.

Grandma was calm. "Let me introduce you, Ruthie dear," she said. Grandma always called her Ruthie when she had something really important to say. "It seems that the wolf is your power animal."

"Is that like a guardian angel?" Red asked.

"Sort of, but more like a spirit friend," said Grandma. "Most people can't see them, but sometimes we can feel them. Hopis believe that our spirit guardians watch over and protect us wherever we go."

The wolf approached and put his paw on
Red's lap. As they touched noses, Red smiled.
"Would you like to stay for lunch?" she asked.

They had a lovely picnic together. The
wolf turned down the carrots and radishes,
but he did eat four tacos after the peppers
were picked out.

Later that day, as the moon began to rise in the east,
they sat together teaching each other their favorite songs.

The End

PS. Spike couldn't sit down for two weeks. We know, because the boys had to come back for a whole month and pull weeds around Grandma's condo. But the best thing is, they never bullied anyone ever again...

PUBLISHING COMPANY, INC.

P.O. Box 1865 ◆ Bellevue, WA 98009
Tel: 425-644-7185 ◆ 888-210-8216 (orders only) ◆ Fax: 425-644-9274
liteinfo@illumin.com ◆ www.illumin.com

Library of Congress Cataloging – in – Publication Data

Wesselman, Henry Barnard.
  Little Ruth Reddingford (and the wolf) : an old tale / retold by Hank Wesselman ;
  illustrated by Raquel Abreu.
     p. cm.
   Summary: When a little girl takes a shortcut to her grandmother's condominium and is set
upon by bullies, Grandma and a mysterious wolf come to her aid.
   ISBN 0-9740190-0-3
   [1. Bullies—Fiction. 2. Grandmothers—Fiction.] I. Lourenco, Raquel, ill. II. Title.

PZ7.W51713Li2004
[E]—dc22

Published in the United States of America
Printed in Singapore by Tien Wah Press
Book Designer: Molly Murrah, Murrah & Company, Kirkland, WA

Illumination Arts Publishing Company is a
member of Publishers in Partnership—replanting our nation's forests.

A portion of the profits from this book will be donated to The Children's Global Foundation, a non-profit organization dedicated to global peace and to helping homeless children worldwide.

This foundation was formed by Children's Global Village (CGV), an organization of leading architects, engineers, developers, builders, and media specialists working together to promote advancements in education and environmentally safe solutions to society's problems. CGV's goal is to develop spiritually-based cities of the future around the world. In addition to futuristic schools, homes, offices and business developments, each city will have a world-class theme park providing culturally diverse education and entertainment. For more information on CGV cities of the future, contact cgv@illumin.com.